Go, Lightning, Go!

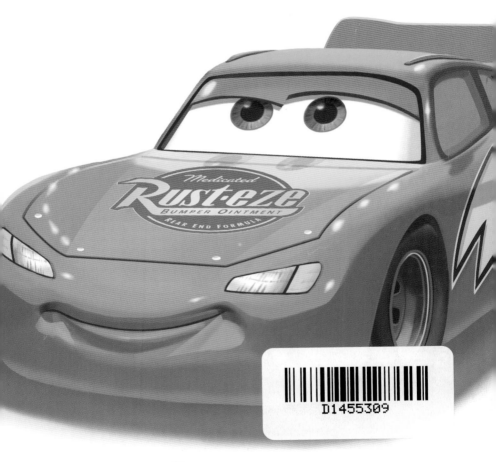

𝒟𝒾𝓈𝓃𝑒𝓎 PRESS
New York • Los Angeles

Lightning went racing.
What did he see?

He saw one cactus
in the desert.

He saw two logs
in the dirt.

He saw three trees
by the road.

He saw four clouds
in the sky.

He saw five cars
on the track.

Go, Lightning, go!